Uncle Noah's Big Boat

Text and Illustrations by Yuki Tsurumi

Judson Press
Valley Forge

Library of Congress Cataloging-in-Publication Data

Tsurumi, Yuki.
  [Noa Ojisan. English]
  Uncle Noah's big boat / text and illustrations by Yuki Tsurumi.
    p. cm.
Based on Genesis 6:13–9:17.
Summary: When Uncle Noah, the carpenter, builds a big boat and gathers every kind of animal inside, he teaches the importance of listening to God and helping one another.
ISBN 0-8170-1336-9 (hardcover)
1. Noah (Biblical figure)—Juvenile fiction. [1. Noah (Biblical figure)—Fiction. 2. Noah's ark—Fiction. 3. Animals—Fiction.] I. Title.
PZ7.T7895Un 1999

[E]—dc21   99-10994

Printed in Japan.
06 05 04 03 02 01 00 99
5 4 3 2 1

Uncle Noah, the carpenter, loved to watch the clouds while he sat and rested.

One day, he heard a voice coming from the sky. It was God speaking to him. "Noah, it will soon start raining hard for many days. All the world — the fields, the mountains, and the cities — will be covered with water. I want you to build a big boat for you and your family. And bring two animals of every kind with you."

Some animals also heard God speaking, and they gathered to help Noah make the big boat.

After a lot of hard work, the boat was finally done. "Welcome aboard!" said Noah and his wife as they greeted all the animals.

The last passengers were a pair of polar bears who had run all the way from the far north sea. After they were all on board, the door was quietly closed.

Noah and his family were tired from all the preparation. The animals were tired, too, especially those who had traveled a long way to Noah and his boat. Soon they all fell into a deep sleep.

Not long after, it started raining quietly outside. Then the rain became heavier and heavier.

"OH, NO!"
The boat rolled back and
forth in the storm.

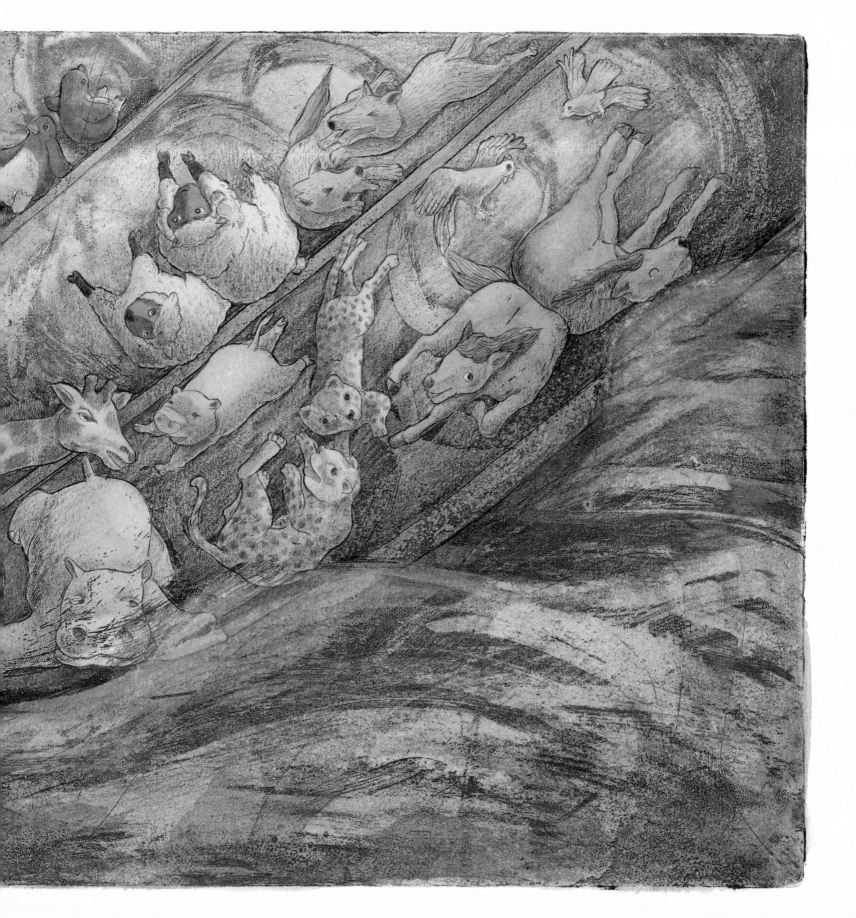

The water was shaking and tossing the boat. "Is our city washed away?" an elephant asked. A wolf cried to his friends who hadn't come onto the boat. But when he listened for an answer, all he heard were the sounds of the rainstorm.

Now everybody understood. They were the only ones left in the world. "Why didn't everyone listen to what God said?" a cow mooed sadly.

Water covered the whole earth. Fields, mountains, and
cities disappeared. There were no flowers, trees, or grass
to be seen anywhere.

And nobody knew where the waves would carry the boat.

Rolling and shaking, creaking and whistling, the boat was tossed about in the rough water.

In the cabin, there was no difference between day and night. It was all the same. "We'll be all right! This is a strong boat." Everybody tried to comfort and cheer up one another.

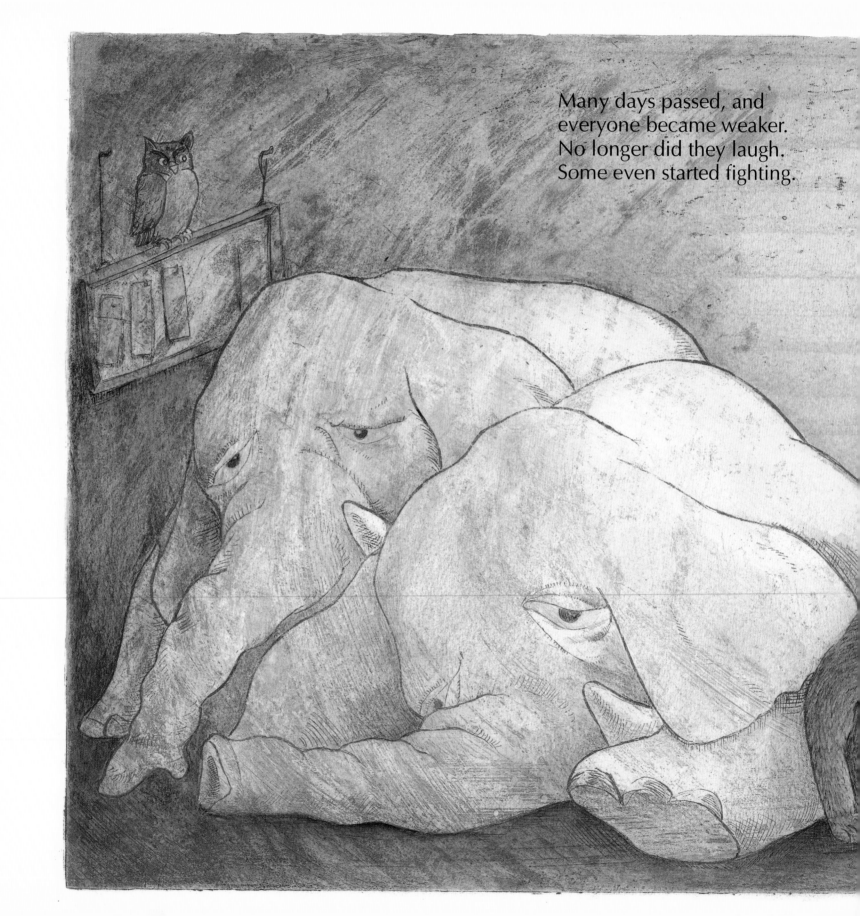

Many days passed, and
everyone became weaker.
No longer did they laugh.
Some even started fighting.

All of a sudden, Noah had an idea! He drew a picture on the wall.

He drew the blue sky, the green forest, the flowers and . . .
"Let me put a white cloud here," said a giraffe. The birds
sang again, and happy smiles returned to everyone's
faces. Noah's wall picture made them feel a lot better.

A few days later, it stopped raining, and they could see the blue sky. Uncle Noah asked a dove to fly away and see what was going on. The dove returned with a twig of green leaves from an olive tree.

"Ah, the water is going away, and the green is coming back!" Noah told the animals.

Finally they landed on top of a mountain. The ground was already dry, and flowers were blooming again.

God promised that everybody would be happy, and he put a rainbow in the sky as a sign of that promise. Everyone's hearts were bright just like the rainbow. The people and animals were as happy as they could be.

"Thank you, God!" said Uncle Noah looking to the sky. Clouds were floating just like they did before.

"That one looks like my big boat," thought Uncle Noah. The fluffy cloud boat was slowly carried away by the wind.

This story is in Genesis 6:13 – 9:17.